NOV 1 0 2005

P9-BYV-415

The Boxcar Children Mysteries

THE CLUE IN THE CORN MAZE

created by
GERTRUDE CHANDLER WARNER

Illustrated by Robert Papp

X
M

ALBERT WHITMAN & Company
Morton Grove, IL

The Clue in the Corn Maze
created by Gertrude Chandler Warner;
illustrated by Robert Papp.

ISBN 0-8075-5556-8 (hardcover)
ISBN 0-8075-5557-6 (paperback)

Cover art by David Cunningham.

For more information about Albert Whitman & Company,
visit our web site at www.albertwhitman.com.

Contents

THE CLUE IN THE
CORN MAZE

CHAPTER 1

Corn, Corn, and More Corn!

"Isn't it amazing?" ten-year-old Violet Alden said as she gazed out the back seat window of the Aldens' rented van. "No matter where you look, all you see is corn, corn and more corn."

"I like corn-on-the-cob," said Benny, Violet's six-year-old brother. "Iowa produces more corn than any other state," their older sister, Jessie, said. Jessie, who was twelve, had read quite a bit about Iowa during their three-hour plane ride from

1

Connecticut that morning.

"Did you know corn is used to make lots of things besides food?" fourteen-year-old Henry Alden piped up from the front seat. "I learned in school that there's corn in fuel, batteries, detergents, and sometimes even clothes."

"Really?" Benny wrinkled his nose. "Is there corn in my shirt?" He stared down at his T-shirt.

"I don't know if there's corn in that particular shirt," Henry said with a laugh. "But I know that cornstarch is used to make the fibers stronger in certain fabrics." Henry was glad he remembered so much from the corn unit.

"All this talk about corn is making me hungry," Benny said as he rubbed his stomach.

"We just had lunch in the airport, Benny," Violet reminded him.

"I know. But I *love* corn-on-the-cob," Benny said. "With butter."

"Well, I'm sure you'll be able to get something to eat soon," Grandfather said, smiling at Benny through the rearview mirror. "We should be arriving at Ken's farm in a few minutes."

Ken Johnson was an old friend of Grandfather's. He had invited James Alden and his grandchildren to visit during the King Corn Days Festival and see his famous corn maze. People came from all over Iowa to see Ken Johnson's corn maze. Each year's maze was bigger and better than the one before it.

"I can't wait to see the corn maze," Violet said eagerly.

"What's a corn maze again?" Benny asked.

"Well, you know what a maze is," Jessie said. "You have a book of mazes at home, remember? A maze is a kind of puzzle where there's a picture and you begin in one of the openings and follow the paths and try to find your way out again."

"And a corn maze is a maze that's cut into a cornfield," Grandfather explained.

"You mean we'll actually get to walk inside the corn maze and find our way out?" Benny asked.

"Yes," Grandfather replied.

"Oh, boy!" Benny squealed with excitement. "I can't wait, either!"

"There's a sign on that fence ahead," Henry said. He pointed at a plain white sign with black lettering that read "Johnson's Corn Maze, Turn Here."

Grandfather turned onto a narrower road. There were no other vehicles in sight. Just fields of corn that stretched as far as the eye could see.

"Mr. Johnson sure lives a long way from town," Violet said.

"And I'm sure he's quite happy about that," Grandfather replied. "Ken never was much of a city person. He likes the wide open space of the country. He likes to be where things are growing. That's why he quit his job all those years ago and bought this farm."

"Look at all those vegetables for sale," Jessie said as they passed a small white farmhouse. There were bins of corn, tomatoes, carrots, onions, cucumbers, beans, and squash spread out across the yard in front of the house. A sign in the driveway read "Peggy's Vegetable Stand."

"Ken said we'd pass a vegetable stand right before we got to his place," Grandfather said. "His house should be the next one."

"There it is!" Benny cried, wiggling in his seat.

Grandfather turned in at the next driveway. He followed the dusty drive that led between a dark red barn and a tall white farmhouse with a huge wrap-around porch.

"Hey, Mr. Johnson has vegetables for sale, too!" Violet pointed at a picnic table that was piled high with cucumbers, beans, tomatoes, and squash.

Grandfather drove around behind the house and parked in front of a wide cornfield. As soon as the van came to a stop, all four doors opened and the Aldens hopped out.

"Is that the corn maze?" Benny stared wide-eyed at the wall of corn in front of him. The corn stood even taller than Grandfather!

"Yes, Benny," Jessie replied. There were two openings into the field. One was marked "Entrance," the other was marked "Exit." But there was a piece of tape stretched across the entrance. The sign that hung from the tape read "Closed Today."

"Closed today?" Violet said. She looked up at the clear blue sky. "But it's such a nice day. Why would the maze be closed?"

"I don't know," Grandfather said.

"Maybe Mr. Johnson is getting the maze ready for the festival on Saturday," Jessie suggested.

"James!" A heavy-set man who was older than Grandfather plodded down the farmhouse steps with his cane. His grin stretched from ear to ear as he greeted the Aldens.

"Ken!" Grandfather exclaimed. "It's so good to see you again!" The two men hugged. Then Grandfather introduced the children.

"It's nice to meet you, Mr. Johnson," Jessie said politely. The four children shook hands with him in turn.

"Please, call me Ken!" He smiled at the children.

"You sure have a nice farm, Ken," Violet said.

Besides the house and barn, there were a couple of large utility buildings, a small white storage shed, and off to the side, a white trailer.

"That trailer reminds me of our boxcar," Benny said.

Henry told Ken how he and the other children had run away before they knew their grandfather because they were afraid he would be mean. They had found an old boxcar in the woods and lived in it for a while.

"But Grandfather found us and we went to live with him," Jessie explained.

"He even moved the boxcar to our house in Greenfield so we can play in it anytime we want," Violet went on.

"Does anybody live in that trailer?" Benny asked Ken.

"Yes, my farmhand, Jack Sweeney," Ken replied. "In fact, there he is over by the barn. Hey, Jack! Come on over and say hello to the Aldens!"

Jack Sweeney was a large, stocky man in his mid-fifties. He wore denim overalls and cowboy boots that were caked with mud. He carried a metal bucket that was full of white toilet paper.

Jack nodded at the Aldens. "Sorry, I've got work to do," he said stiffly. Then he went into the barn.

Ken frowned slightly as he leaned on his cane. "You'll have to excuse Jack. We had some vandalism last night and he's trying to get things cleaned up."

"Vandalism?" Benny asked. "What's vandalism?"

"It's when someone damages another person's property on purpose," Jessie explained.

"Someone wound toilet paper all through the maze," Ken said. "They made quite a mess. We had to close down for the day in order to get it all cleaned up."

"That's terrible!" Jessie exclaimed. "Who would do such a thing?"

"I don't know," Ken replied. "Somebody who wants me to cancel the King Corn Days Festival this weekend. Look what else we found." Ken reached into his pocket and pulled out a crumpled sheet of paper. The paper contained a bunch of letters that had been cut out of magazines and newspapers and arranged on the paper to read CANCEL THE FESTIVAL.

"Jack found this in the center of the maze," Ken explained.

"Why would someone want to stop the King Corn Days Festival?" Grandfather asked.

"It's a mystery," Ken replied.

"We're good at solving mysteries," Benny spoke up as Jack Sweeney came out of the barn with an empty bucket. Jack had a stern look on his face.

"Maybe we could look around in the maze and see if we can find some clues," Henry offered.

"No!" Jack said, blocking the entrance to the maze. "You kids stay out of there."

"Jack's been working hard cleaning up

the maze all day," Ken said apologetically. "Let's let him finish. Once he's done, you kids can go in there."

"We could help you clean up, Mr. Sweeney," Jessie offered. "Then you'll get done a little sooner."

"I don't need any help," Mr. Sweeney said gruffly.

"Why don't you all bring your things inside," Ken said, leading them away from the cornfield. "Are you hungry? I baked a couple of blueberry pies this morning."

"Blueberry pie?" Benny's eyes lit up. "Oh, boy!"

"Ken has always been a wonderful cook," Grandfather said.

Ken smiled. "After we've had some pie, I'll show you around the farm. Maybe by then Jack will be done working and you can see the maze."

Jack muttered something under his breath, then lumbered back into the maze.

"It seems strange that Mr. Sweeney wouldn't want some help cleaning up all that toilet paper," Jessie said as she and

Henry lagged behind the others.

Henry shrugged. "He's probably got his own system for getting things done. Maybe he thought we'd just get in his way."

CHAPTER 2

The Corn Maze

After the Aldens unpacked, Ken showed them around the farm. He led them past chickens, goats, horses, even a llama.

The llama was white with tan spots. He had a long, graceful neck, thin legs, and curious brown eyes.

Ken went over and stroked the llama's neck. "This is Sunny," Ken said with a smile. "He's very gentle. Would you kids like to pet him?"

"Sure," Violet said right away. The Aldens crowded around Ken and reached out to pet the llama.

Sunny seemed to enjoy the attention.

"His fur feels like wool," Benny said. His hand was buried in the thick fur.

"It *is* wool," Ken replied. "You can use llama wool for knitting or weaving. During the festival on Saturday, we'll even show people how to do that."

"I'd love to try knitting," said Violet. She enjoyed working with her hands.

"We'll also have hayrides and pony rides and games," Ken said.

"What kind of games?" Grandfather asked.

"Horseshoe and some relay races. And we'll set up a mini maze with bales of straw for the younger children. Maybe you all would like to help with that?"

"We'd love to help," Jessie said. "This festival sounds fun."

"It is fun. And of course there will be the usual 'all you can eat' corn-on-the-cob, too."

"All you can eat?" Benny's eyes lit up.

"Oh, boy! This is my kind of festival!"

Everyone laughed.

Jack Sweeney came around behind the barn. "I'm finished cleaning up, so I suppose those kids can go in the maze now." He eyed the children warily.

"Thanks, Jack," Ken said. Then he turned to the Aldens. "What do you say? Would you like to explore the maze?"

"Oh, yes!" they exclaimed.

"Can we, Grandfather?" Violet asked.

"Sure," Grandfather replied.

They all walked back around the barn. Ken pulled down the tape that was blocking the entrance. Then he grabbed a tall stick with a white cloth tied to the end of it and handed it to Jessie.

"James and I will watch you from that lookout over there." With his cane, he pointed to a wooden structure that looked like a clubhouse with stairs. "If you run into trouble or you need help finding your way out, raise your stick and I'll direct you."

"Okay," Jessie said.

Ken handed Henry a sheet of paper.

"Here's a map of the maze," he said.

Benny stood on tiptoe to see the map. "It looks like an eagle!"

Ken smiled proudly. "Yes, all my mazes form a picture. This year's picture is of an eagle."

"That's neat," said Violet.

Henry folded up the map and tucked it in his back pocket. "We'll try and find our way without the map first," he said.

The other Aldens nodded in agreement.

"We're good at solving mazes," Jessie said.

"I'm glad to hear that," Ken said.

"Have fun!" Grandfather called as the children hurried over to the maze entrance.

"We will!" Benny waved. But his smile faded when he noticed Mr. Sweeney scowling at them from over by the barn.

The sun felt warm beating down on the children's backs as they went deeper into the maze. The ground was rock-hard beneath their feet. Rich green cornstalks towered over them. The stalks were as wide around as small tree trunks. They were so close together that not even Benny could sneak between the rows. Each stalk had several silky ears of corn sticking out like small arms.

"Mmm! The corn is so fresh you can almost smell it growing," Violet said as they turned a corner.

Jessie stepped forward and sniffed an ear of corn. "I think you're right, Violet," she laughed.

"Which way should we go?" Benny asked when they came to a fork in the path.

"This way." Violet pointed. She started off down the path that led to the right. The others stuck close to her heels. But that path soon turned out to be a dead end, so they turned around. When they arrived back at the fork, Violet and Benny started to turn to the left.

"Are you sure that's the right way?" Henry scratched his head. "I think that way leads back to the maze entrance."

Jessie rested her stick in the crook of her arm and looked first one direction, then the other. "Yes, we turned right when we turned off this main path. But then we turned around, so now we have to go right again."

For the next hour, the Aldens followed path after path. Some of the paths led into large open areas. Others ended abruptly in dead ends.

The children noticed a few leftover bits of toilet paper stuck to some of the plants. Henry grabbed one of the larger pieces and peered at it. "I wonder if we can use this to figure out who toilet-papered the maze?"

"How?" Benny asked. "It's just plain old toilet paper. Everybody has toilet paper."

"Yes, but not all toilet paper is the same," Jessie pointed out.

Violet looked closely at the piece. "That's true. See all the dots that are pressed into it? They form a swirly design."

"You're right, Violet," Jessie said. "I bet every brand of toilet paper has its own design."

"This piece could be an important clue," Henry said as he stuffed the toilet paper into his pocket.

The Aldens kept walking. They didn't find any other clues, but they enjoyed winding through the maze. A few minutes later, they reached the exit. Grandfather and Ken were waiting for them.

"You did it!" Grandfather clapped his hands together. "You found your way out."

"Did you need the map?" Ken asked as Jessie handed him her stick.

Henry patted his back pocket, where he'd put Ken's map. "Nope. We never took it out once."

"You kids are very good at solving mazes indeed!" Ken said with a smile. "Shall we go in the house and see what we can put together for supper?"

"Oh, yes!" said Benny. The children were eager to wash up and help make supper.

"So, how do you build a corn maze, Ken?" Henry asked as they started across the yard.

"Well, the first step is to figure out what picture I want the maze to form. Then I use a computer to help me draw it out. When the corn is about six inches tall, I cut the maze paths. Then it's just a matter of maintaining the field and waiting for the visitors to come."

"That's really interesting," Violet said. "I'd like to plan a maze."

"Maybe one day you will," Ken said. "Hey, it looks like we've got company." The Aldens' van was now parked between a rusty blue pickup and a sparkling-clean gray sedan.

The children clattered up the back porch steps. Jessie held the door for Ken.

"David? Kurt? Are you here?" Ken called. His cane tapped against the linoleum floor as he turned into the kitchen. The Aldens followed.

A dark-haired, thirty-five-year-old man dressed in a business suit and tie was reading a financial magazine at the kitchen table.

An older man with curly white hair stood by the stove stirring something in a large pot of boiling water. It smelled like corn.

"Hello! You must be the Aldens." The younger man stood up and shook Grandfather's hand. "I'm Ken's son, David."

"Pleased to meet you," Grandfather said. Then he introduced his grandchildren.

The older man smiled. "I'm Kurt, Ken's much better looking younger brother," he said with a wide grin that showed a gap between his top two front teeth.

The Aldens laughed as they shook hands with Kurt.

Ken scowled. "What brings you around, Kurt? Checking up on me again?"

"No," Kurt said. "I brought you some freshly picked sweet corn. This corn was still growing in my field about fifteen minutes ago."

"Wow, that is freshly picked!" said Henry.

"Corn on the cob is best if you don't pick it until you've got the water boiling and you're ready to drop the ears into the pot," Kurt said. "So I rushed right over and put the pot on the stove."

"Why did you bring your own corn when Ken has so much right here?" Benny asked.

Kurt smiled. "Well, I'll tell you, Benny.

Ken can build a corn maze so spectacular that people will come from all over Iowa to see it. But you wouldn't want to eat his corn! My corn is at least fit for eating."

"That's because you grow sweet corn," Ken pointed out. "I grow field corn."

"What did I tell you?" Kurt leaned toward Benny. "Would you want to eat the same kind of corn the cows eat?" he asked.

Benny quickly shook his head.

Kurt dipped a pair of tongs into the boiling pot and pulled out a steaming ear of corn-on-the-cob. He set it on a plate to cool.

"Let me put a little butter on this corn and then we'll see what you think. Okay, Benny?" Kurt said as he grabbed the butter dish and a knife.

"Okay," Benny said, his mouth watering.

The butter melted on the corn as fast as Kurt could spread it. Kurt added a little salt, then handed the plate to Benny.

"Now you tell me, have you ever tasted better corn-on-the-cob?" Kurt asked. He watched Benny's face anxiously.

Benny picked up the corn and took a big bite. "Mmm!" he cried, his eyes wide with amazement. "This is the best corn-on-the-cob I've ever had!"

"Let's get some more plates," Kurt said. "There's plenty for everyone."

While Kurt dished up the corn, David started talking to Ken. "So, Dad," he said carefully. "Uncle Kurt told me about the trouble in the maze today. I hope you weren't out there working in the hot sun."

"I wish my brother would mind his own business," Ken said with a pointed look at Kurt. "I'm perfectly capable of doing a little work in my own field."

"But Dad. Your arthritis!" David said.

"My arthritis is fine. Besides, Jack did most of the work."

David took a deep breath. "I know you don't want to hear this. But it seems to me the maze and the King Corn Days Festival are getting to be an awful lot of work."

Ken scowled. "We've had this argument before. I'm not selling the farm and I'm not moving into town with you and Linda."

"You're not as young as you used to be, Pops," David said. "This is getting to be too much for you."

"I'll decide when something's too much for me," Ken said stiffly. "Now we're not going to talk about this anymore. Are you staying for supper, David?"

David sighed. "Yes. Linda's got a meeting tonight, so I'll stay."

"Good." Ken nodded. "Then why don't you go fire up the grill. I'll take some hamburgers out of the freezer. We can have hamburgers and fresh garden salads with our corn." He got up and shuffled into the other room with his cane.

"I know how much Dad loves this farm and the festival," David said to the Aldens once Ken was gone. "But it scares me to think about someone prowling around the maze with toilet paper and leaving threatening notes. If this is going to keep up, I'm afraid I'm going to have to insist that Dad give up the farm."

"I think that would just about break his heart," Grandfather said.

"I know," David admitted. He looked sad. "But what else can I do? I don't want him to get hurt."

"Don't worry," Henry said. "We'll figure out who vandalized the maze and wrote that note. And we'll get them to stop."

"For my father's sake, I hope you can," David said.

CHAPTER 3

Yuck!

Violet woke up during the
night. She was thirsty, so she decided to go
down to the kitchen to get a drink of
water.

She slipped quietly out of bed. As she
crept across the room, something out the
window caught her eye.

Violet tiptoed over to the window and
peered out into the darkness. She saw a
round white light bobbing through the
cornfield. Was it a flashlight? Was somebody
in the maze in the middle of the night?

"Jessie!" Violet whispered. She hurried over to the other bed and gently shook her sister's shoulder. "Jessie, wake up! I think there's someone in the corn maze."

Jessie rubbed her eyes and rolled toward Violet. "What?" she said sleepily.

"There's a light in the corn maze," Violet hissed. "I think someone's in there."

Jessie tossed her covers aside and followed Violet over to the window. But now, when the girls looked, the light was gone.

"That's strange," Violet said.

"Are you sure you saw a light in the field?" Jessie asked. "There's a light on inside Mr. Sweeney's trailer. Maybe that's what you saw?"

Violet couldn't remember whether there had been a light on in Mr. Sweeney's trailer when she looked before, but she was sure she'd seen another light in the field.

"The light I saw was moving," Violet said. "It was bobbing up and down—the way it would if someone was carrying a flashlight."

A moment later the light in Mr. Sweeney's

trailer went out. Everything was dark.

"Maybe it was just Mr. Sweeney checking to make sure no one was in the maze," Jessie suggested. "He probably didn't see anything, so he went back to bed."

"You're probably right, Jessie," Violet agreed. "I'm sorry I woke you."

"That's okay," Jessie said. "Let's try and get some sleep."

The next morning, Ken had stacks of pancakes and a frying pan full of sausages ready when the Aldens came downstairs.

"You shouldn't have gone to so much trouble, Ken," Grandfather said.

"Why not?" Ken asked. "I love to cook. Always have. You know that. Now eat up, before everything gets cold."

"Okay," Benny said as he slid into a chair. Grandfather, Henry, Jessie, and Violet sat down, too.

Benny helped himself to several pancakes. A warm breeze blew through the open kitchen window. The Aldens could tell it was going to be another hot day.

A strange odor caught Benny's attention.

"What's that smell?" he asked, wrinkling his nose.

"It must be pancakes," Henry answered. "You sure have a lot of them on your plate."

"No," Benny shook his head. "I know how pancakes smell. This is something else. Something that doesn't smell very good."

Violet sniffed. "I smell it, too."

"Me, too," Jessie said.

Ken set a plate of toast on the table. "I think what you all are smelling is fresh manure," Ken said. "I'm afraid that's not an unusual smell when you live in the country. But you get used to it."

There was a knock at the back door and Jack Sweeney poked his head inside. "Ken?" he said in a serious voice. "We've got a problem."

"What is it?" Ken asked.

"Come outside," Mr. Sweeney said. He was dressed in overalls and the same muddy cowboy boots he had worn the day before.

Ken grabbed his cane and followed Mr. Sweeney. The Aldens went outside, too. Mr. Sweeney glared at the children, but said nothing. He led them all down the porch steps and out toward the corn maze. The smell of manure was getting stronger. It was so strong that Benny pinched his nose shut.

Mr. Sweeney stopped at the entrance to the maze. The maze path was completely buried under a layer of manure.

"Oh!" Jessie gasped.

"A little manure helps things grow," Ken said. "But this is more than a little manure. People who come to visit the maze aren't going to want to wade through this. Is it all through the maze?"

"'Fraid so," Mr. Sweeney replied. "It'll take a while to shovel it all out and then spread hay over the paths. Looks like you're going to have to close up the maze a second time." But Mr. Sweeney didn't look very disappointed. In fact, he almost looked happy.

"We can help you clean it up, Mr. Sweeney," Henry offered.

"Of course we can," Jessie put in. "You don't want to close the maze two days in a row."

"I don't want a bunch of kids tromping through a maze full of manure, Ken," Mr. Sweeney said. "They'll just make more work for me."

"No, we won't," Benny said.

"I assure you, Mr. Sweeney, these children are very good workers," Grandfather said. "With their help, I'm sure you'll be able to open on time, Ken."

"It's settled then." Ken banged his cane on the ground. "Let's finish our breakfast. You're welcome to join us, Jack."

"I've already eaten," Mr. Sweeney said coldly.

"After breakfast, we'll find some old clothes, gloves, and shoes for you all," Ken told the Aldens. "Then you can help Jack clean things up. With a little luck, the maze will open on schedule today."

Once the Aldens were dressed for cleaning up manure, Mr. Sweeney passed out shovels and a wheelbarrow. Then he showed them where to dump the manure.

"I may use it for the garden later," Mr. Sweeney explained.

Then he led the children back to the maze. "I've been working on the path straight ahead," Mr. Sweeney said. "Why don't you kids work the paths that go off over there? I haven't been down that way." Mr. Sweeney gestured toward the right.

"Okay," the Aldens agreed.

Before Mr. Sweeney turned to leave, Violet told him about the light she'd seen moving through the maze during the night.

"Jessie and I also saw a light on in your place, Mr. Sweeney," Violet said. "So we know you were up. Did you see anything unusual?"

"Nope," Mr. Sweeney said.

"What were you doing up in the middle of the night?" Jessie asked. "Did you go outside to check on the maze?"

Mr. Sweeney looked annoyed. "No. I got up to use the bathroom. Then I went right back to bed. Same as every other night."

"So maybe the person who spread the manure was carrying the light," Henry said. "Do you know anyone who would want to sabotage the corn maze?"

"Can't think of anyone," Mr. Sweeney replied. "Look, I really don't have time for all these questions," he said. "There's a lot of work to be done. Now, I thought you kids wanted to help."

"We do," Violet said. "But we also want to figure out who's been making such a mess in the maze."

"We're good at solving mysteries," Henry said.

"Well, right now I need kids who are good at cleaning things up rather than kids who are good at solving mysteries." He set off down the maze path.

"I don't think Mr. Sweeney likes us very much," Benny said after the older man had left.

"He sure doesn't like us asking questions," Henry said. "Do you think he could have anything to do with the vandalism?"

"Why would he vandalize Ken's maze?" Violet asked. "It looks like he's the one who ends up doing most of the cleanup."

"Plus, he and Ken are friends," Benny said. "He works for Ken. And he lives right by Ken, on his land!"

"Well, he sure isn't very friendly," Jessie put in. "But maybe that's just because he's had a lot of extra work to do lately."

"Speaking of work, we'd better get started," Henry said as he grabbed the handles of the wheelbarrow.

The Aldens started down the main path, then followed the path that veered off to the right.

"Yuck," Benny said, stepping gingerly. This is disgusting!" He jabbed his shovel into a pile of manure and plopped it into the wheelbarrow.

"Wait a minute!" Violet said. "Look! There are footprints over here."

"Mr. Sweeney said he hasn't been down this path yet," Henry said. "So the footprints must belong to the person who made all this mess."

The footprints were long and narrow and pointed at the tip.

"They look like prints from cowboy boots," Violet said.

"You could be right, Violet," Jessie said.

"Mr. Sweeney had on cowboy boots," Benny pointed out.

"I bet a lot of people who live around here wear cowboy boots," Violet said.

"Violet's right," Henry said. "We don't want to jump to any wrong conclusions."

"Besides," Violet put in. "It's possible Mr. Sweeney did come down this path after all. Maybe he just didn't remember."

For the next couple of hours, the Aldens mucked out the maze paths and dumped the manure in the pile behind the storage shed.

"There sure are a lot of paths in this maze," Jessie said as she wiped the back of her hand across her sweaty forehead.

Not every path was covered in manure, but the Aldens went down every path anyway. Cleaning up manure was hot, dirty work. But the important thing was getting the maze ready so Ken could open in the afternoon.

"Hey, what's that?" Benny asked when they turned another corner. Something red lay in the dirt up ahead. Benny ran to see what it was.

"It's a cap," Benny said, picking it up.

"Not just a cap," Jessie said. "It's a cap that has a built-in flashlight. Look." She flipped a tiny switch on the side of the cap and a bulb lit up.

"Wow! That's pretty cool!" Benny exclaimed.

"I knew I'd seen a light in the maze last night," Violet cried.

"Good work, Benny," Henry said. "Whoever was in here last night probably dropped it."

Mr. Sweeney came to check on them a few minutes later. "How are you kids doing?" he asked.

"Pretty good," Jessie said. "We're almost done with all the paths on this side of the maze."

"Good." Mr. Sweeney nodded.

"Mr. Sweeney?" Benny held up the cap he'd found. "We found this while we were working. Do you know who it belongs to?"

Mr. Sweeney squinted at the cap in Benny's hand. "It's not mine."

"Does it belong to Ken?" Violet asked.

"Don't know," Mr. Sweeney replied. "You'd have to ask him."

"No, it's not my cap," Ken said later when the Aldens showed the cap to him. "Where did you find it?"

"We found it inside the maze," Henry said.

"We're wondering if it belongs to the person who dumped the manure there," Jessie added.

Ken frowned. "I wish I knew who that was."

"You don't have any idea?" Grandfather asked.

"Not a clue," Ken replied. "But I'll tell you something. No one is going to scare me into canceling the festival. The King Corn Days Festival must go on!" He pounded his fist on the table.

"Yeah!" shouted Benny.

CHAPTER 4

Open for Business

The Aldens got cleaned up and changed clothes. Then Jessie and Violet made sandwiches for lunch.

"Could I watch the people in the maze from the lookout tower?" Benny asked as he set the table.

"Sure, Benny," Ken answered. "If anybody gets lost, you can direct them out."

"Oh, boy!" Benny clapped his hands.

"In fact, the rest of you can help, too, if you want," Ken said. "I could use a couple of ticket-takers. And sometimes people want to buy vegetables. It can get pretty busy if a lot of customers come at the same time."

"We'd love to help," Violet said as she carried a plate of sandwiches to the table. Jessie carried a pitcher of lemonade. Then everyone sat down to eat.

"Oh, before I forget," Ken reached into his shirt pocket and pulled out an envelope. "The mail carrier delivered this to the wrong house. This letter should go to Peggy Rodman, my neighbor down the street. You would have passed her place on your way here."

"Is that the house with all the vegetables out front?" Henry asked.

"Yes," Ken answered. He handed the letter to Henry. "Would you kids mind delivering this letter to her after lunch? I can take care of the visitors until you get back."

Henry took the letter. "Sure, Ken. We'd be happy to."

The Aldens walked along the side of the road to get to Peggy Rodman's place. Corn grew tall in the field beside them.

As soon as the Aldens started up the gravel drive that led to Peggy Rodman's house, a black dog leaped against the kennel beside the garage and barked.

"Quiet, Rosie!" a woman said from her chair on the porch. The dog immediately quieted down.

The woman stood up when she noticed the children. She was around David's age, with chin-length blond hair. She wore a plaid shirt, faded jeans, and tennis shoes.

"Can I help you?" the woman asked cheerfully as the Aldens approached. "Are you here to buy some vegetables?"

There were bins of carrots, onions, cucumbers, beans, corn, and several kinds of squash spread out on the grassy front lawn. The vegetables took up most of her yard. Up close, some of them didn't look very good. Several had rotten spots. They must have been sitting out for a long time.

"No," Henry said. "We're looking for Ms. Peggy Rodman."

"I'm Peggy," the woman said.

Henry handed Peggy the letter. "We're

staying with Ken Johnson. This letter was delivered to him by mistake, so he asked us to bring it to you."

"Oh." Peggy's smile disappeared when Henry mentioned Ken's name. "Well, thank you for bringing it down here," she said stiffly.

"It was no trouble," Jessie said.

Peggy turned to walk away, but Benny called after her. "Have you seen Ken's corn maze yet?"

Peggy stopped. She looked a little surprised by Benny's question. "No," she said slowly. "And I probably never will see it."

"Why not?" Violet asked.

Peggy seemed a little embarrassed. "Well, I'm afraid Mr. Johnson and I don't get along very well," she said.

The Aldens looked at each other. Ken was so nice. Why wouldn't he and Peggy get along?

"Did you know there's been trouble with Ken's maze this week?" Jessie asked.

"Yes, I heard he had to close yesterday. One of my customers said there had been some vandalism the night before."

"That's right," Jessie said. "Somebody toilet-papered the whole maze."

"What a shame," Peggy said.

"And last night someone dumped a whole bunch of manure in it," Benny said, holding his nose.

"Well, I didn't hear anything about that," Peggy said.

"You're Ken's closest neighbor," Henry said. "Did you happen to wake up at all during the night either last night or the night before? Did you hear or see anything suspicious?"

"I slept like a baby both nights," Peggy said. "Now, if you don't mind, I have work to do." She turned and headed back to her house.

"Before we go," Benny said, "Do you think I could use your bathroom?" He seemed a little uncomfortable.

Peggy looked sympathetic. "Sure," she said, motioning for the children to follow her. "Come on. I'll show you where it is."

The other children waited on the front

porch for Benny. He didn't take very long.

"Thanks," he called to Peggy when he was finished. Then they all headed back toward Ken's house.

Along the way, Benny pulled a scrap of toilet paper out of his pocket and handed it to Henry.

"Where did you get that?" Henry asked.

"From Peggy's bathroom," Benny replied. "I was wondering if it was the same as the toilet paper we found in the maze."

The other children examined the scrap. "It's got the same swirly pattern of raised dots," Violet pointed out.

"Just because Peggy uses the same kind of toilet paper we found in the maze doesn't mean she's the one who toilet-papered it." Henry said. "We have no reason to suspect her."

"She said she and Ken don't get along," Benny said.

"That still doesn't prove she's the vandal," Jessie said.

Benny's face fell.

"But it was good thinking to try to match

up the toilet paper," Jessie said quickly.

"That's right," Henry put in. "We just need more evidence before we can figure out who vandalized Ken's maze."

For the rest of the afternoon, the Aldens helped with the maze. Jessie helped Ken run the cash register. Violet and Henry took tickets. And Benny and Grandfather watched from the lookout.

"It's just as much fun watching people go through the maze as it is going through ourselves," Benny said, resting his elbows on the ledge.

There were a lot of visitors. Many of them said they had tried to come yesterday and were disappointed the maze was closed.

"I'm glad you're open today," one lady said as she followed a curly-haired little boy over to the goats. "A couple hours out here and Daniel will be ready for a nap."

"Are these vegetables for sale?" another lady called from the front yard.

"Yes, they are," Ken called back.

"I see you took my advice this year," a third lady said to Ken as she plopped two bags of beans down on the table in front of Jessie.

"What advice was that?" Ken asked.

"I'm the one who suggested you join up with that lady down the street," the woman said. "It's nice to be able to go through your maze and then buy our fresh vegetables right here without having to stop at her place, too."

"Oh, I remember you now," Ken grinned. "Yes, I did take your advice. Or, at least I tried to. Unfortunately, my neighbor wasn't interested in going into business together, so I just planted a small vegetable patch myself."

"Well, I'm glad you did," the woman said as she took some money out of her billfold and handed it to Jessie.

"So am I," said the next woman in line. "Your vegetables look wonderful! And they're cheaper than your neighbor's."

When all the customers were busy feeding the animals or working their way through the maze, Henry asked, "Why wouldn't Peggy want to go into business with you, Ken? It seems like it would be a good arrangement for both of you. You've got the maze and she's got the vegetables."

"That's what I thought, too, Henry," Ken said. "But she didn't want to haul all her vegetables up here. And I think she believed she could make more money selling her vegetables herself."

"I wonder if she really is making more money," Jessie said. "A lot of people are buying your vegetables. But when we were down at her place earlier, she didn't have any customers."

"Well, she's got more vegetables for sale than I do," Ken said. "Selling vegetables was just an experiment for me this year. I didn't plant a very large patch. When I run out, people will have to buy from her again."

"Hey, Ken," Jack Sweeney called as he lumbered toward them. He did not look happy. "We've got to get a lock on that storage shed. I've been shooing people out of there all afternoon." He put his hands on his hips and glared at the people who were entering the maze.

"Oh, I don't think there's anything in the storage shed that we need worry about," Ken said, unconcerned.

"There are tools in there. And animal feed," Mr. Sweeney said. "I just caught a bunch of kids climbing all over the bags of feed. Their parents weren't paying any attention to what their children were doing!" He sounded pretty angry.

"All right, Jack. Calm down," Ken said. "We'll get a lock the next time either of us goes into town."

Mr. Sweeney didn't look satisfied. "You know, I didn't take this job to be a baby-sitter," he said as he took his hat off and rubbed his forehead. "I'm a farmhand. That's what I do."

"I know, Jack," Ken said sympathetically. "And you're very good at what you do. You've been with me almost twenty years, and I've never been unhappy with your work."

Mr. Sweeney looked away as though he were embarrassed by the compliment.

"I know you wish I'd never started the King Corn Days Festival," Ken continued. "I know you don't like having all these strangers milling around. But I love the festival! I love planning a new maze each year. I love building it and caring for it and sharing my love of farming with all the people who come to see it."

Mr. Sweeney didn't say anything.

Ken took a slow, deep breath. "I won't give up the festival, but I'll see that these people don't interfere with your work anymore. Okay, Jack?"

Mr. Sweeney nodded. He put his hat back on his head. "I'd appreciate that," he said as he walked away.

CHAPTER 5

The Argument

"So, who'd like to go on a quick hayride before supper?" Ken asked after the last customer had gone home and the maze was closed for the day.

"A hayride! Oh, boy!" Benny cried, jumping up and down.

Ken led the Aldens back over to the barn. There was a large green tractor parked there. A trailer with bales of hay was hitched to the tractor.

"Climb aboard!" Ken said.

"Hey, this looks like fun!" Jessie said. She

hopped up onto the trailer.

"It sure does," Violet agreed. "But where do we sit?"

"On the hay," Ken said with a laugh. "That's why they call it a hayride."

The Aldens laughed, too.

Grandfather helped Benny onto the trailer, then turned to Ken, who was climbing awkwardly onto the tractor seat. "Can I help you there, Ken?" Grandfather asked.

"No, no," Ken waved his hand. "I'm fine." He started the tractor, and with a quick lurch, they were off.

Ken drove the Aldens all around his property. It wasn't a fast ride, but it was a lot of fun.

"This land is really quite hilly," Grandfather noted. "I always think of the Midwest as being flat."

"Parts of Iowa are flat, but we've got some gentle rolling hills around here," Ken said with a smile. "Isn't it beautiful?"

"It sure is," Grandfather agreed.

Ken drove along the edge of his cornfield, then turned down a narrow, rutted road. The road led to the top of a ridge, then down to a small lake. Mr. Sweeney was sitting by the lake. As the group drew closer, they could see he was cutting pieces out of a newspaper.

"Hey, Jack," Ken said. "What are you doing?"

Ken quickly gathered up the newspaper scraps. "I-I-I'm uh, just t-t-taking a little break," he stammered. "I have a nephew who lives in California now, but he likes to keep up with the local sports coverage. So I'm clipping articles."

"Well, we won't disturb you," Ken said. He turned the tractor in a wide circle and drove back up the hill.

When they got back to the utility barn, Ken parked the tractor.

"Thank you for taking us on a hayride, Ken," Jessie said.

"You're welcome, Jessie," Ken replied. Then he and Grandfather went inside to start supper. The children decided to stay outside and look at the animals. Benny especially wanted to visit Sunny, the llama.

While they were petting Sunny, Benny noticed a scrap from an empty feed bag lying on the ground. He picked it up.

"Does anybody know where there's a garbage can?" Benny asked.

"There's one over by Mr. Sweeney's trailer," Violet said, pointing.

Benny skipped over to the garbage. He lifted the lid and was surprised to find the entire can full of empty toilet paper rolls and plastic wrapping from Softee brand toilet paper.

"Hey, come look at this!" he called to the other kids.

They came over and peered into the garbage can.

"I wonder if all of this came from the toilet paper in the maze?" Jessie asked.

"I bet it did," Violet said. "Look!" She pointed to a cardboard roll that still had a little toilet paper attached to it. "This is the same swirly pattern we saw on the toilet paper we found in the maze."

"And the paper at Peggy Rodman's," Benny added.

Just then, Mr. Sweeney came up behind them. "What do you kids think you're doing digging in my garbage?" he asked.

Mr. Sweeney's tone of voice startled Benny so much that he dropped the metal lid. "I was just throwing some garbage away," he said.

Henry picked the lid up and replaced it on the garbage can. "We couldn't help but notice all the toilet paper rolls and packaging," Henry said.

"This is the only garbage can around here. The person who wound all that toilet paper through the maze must have put the garbage here," Mr. Sweeney said gruffly. He checked the garbage can lid to make sure it was secure. "I suppose that's better than leaving it in the maze."

Mr. Sweeney brushed past the children and thudded up the steps to his trailer. "Please find someplace else to play," he said. "And don't dig in the garbage."

"Okay, Mr. Sweeney," Henry said. "We're sorry we bothered you."

"Mr. Sweeney doesn't like us," Benny

grumbled as they headed back toward Ken's house. "He's mean."

"I don't think he realized Benny had picked up some trash," Jessie said. "Instead he got mad at us for digging in his garbage."

"Maybe he got mad because he didn't want us to see all the toilet paper rolls and plastic wrapping," Henry said.

"Why would he care about what we saw in his garbage?" Jessie asked. "Unless he's the one who put all the toilet paper and manure in the maze?"

"That seems kind of strange when he's the one who has to clean up the mess," Violet said.

"Still, I think we should keep an eye on Mr. Sweeney," Henry said.

The others nodded in agreement.

The children went inside the house and found David pacing back and forth in the kitchen. His dress shirt was unbuttoned and his tie was loose. He looked upset.

"Why didn't you tell me, Dad?" David demanded.

"I just did," Ken replied calmly as he checked the casserole in the oven.

David frowned. "I mean, why didn't you tell me as soon as you discovered the manure in the maze?"

"What difference does it make when I tell you?" Ken asked.

"I could have come over and helped with the cleanup," David replied.

"Don't be silly," Ken said. He sat down at the table next to Grandfather. "You can't leave your job at the bank every time I have a little problem."

"That sounds like a big problem to me," David said. "You know I don't like you working in the fields, Dad. You're not a young man anymore."

"So you keep telling me," Ken muttered. "But I assure you I wasn't working in the fields. Jack and the Aldens did all of the work."

"That's true, David," Violet piped up. "We helped Mr. Sweeney."

"We didn't want Ken to work too hard, either," Henry added.

The back door burst open. "Hello, everyone!" Kurt said as he came into the kitchen carrying two brown bags that were overflowing with corn.

"Oh, boy! Did you bring us more corn, Kurt?" Benny squealed with excitement.

"I sure did, Benny," Kurt smiled. He set the bags on the counter.

"Hooray!" Benny jumped up and down.

"Did you hear there was some more trouble with that maze this morning, Uncle Kurt?" David asked.

"Yes, I did."

Ken whirled around. "Who told you?"

"Jack did. Just now. Honestly, Ken. Farming is hard enough by itself, especially with your arthritis. I don't know why you bother with this maze, too."

"Because I enjoy it," Ken said. "If I have to give up my maze, I may as well give up the whole farm and move into town with David and his wife."

"That's not such a terrible idea, Dad," David said.

"Listen to your son, Ken," Kurt said. "I

really think that once the King Corn Days Festival is behind us, we should sit down with our lawyers and work out some sort of deal. I'd like to buy you out."

"You don't have the money to buy me out," Ken said.

Kurt and David exchanged a look. "Well, Ken," Kurt said carefully. "I went to see somebody at the bank about getting a loan."

Ken opened his mouth, but no words came out.

"I think I could swing it," Kurt went on.

"No," Ken said, shaking his head.

Kurt pulled out a chair next to Ken and sat down. "You don't have to sell the house. Just sell me the land. Let me farm it."

"No!"

Kurt leaned back in his chair. "You're being stubborn!" he declared.

"It's my land!" Ken exclaimed. "I can be stubborn with my own land if I want to be."

"Think of your health, Dad," David pleaded. "If Kurt wants to buy you out, I think you should at least consider it."

"You can still be involved," Kurt

promised. "I'd take your advice. Just let me
handle the hard work."

"If you keep pestering me, I'll sell to
Peggy Rodman instead of you," Ken threat-
ened.

Kurt looked stunned. "You wouldn't," he
said.

"Why wouldn't I?" Ken asked. "She
made me an offer a few months ago. A
pretty good one, I might add."

"B-but," Kurt stammered, clearly upset.
"She's never liked either one of us. Why
would you sell to her instead of to your own
flesh and blood?"

"Because at one time, all this land belonged to her family," Ken explained. "I
bought this farm from her dad, you know.
Letting her buy it back might go a long way
toward mending fences between us."

Kurt was so angry the Aldens could almost see smoke coming out of his ears. "If
you sell to her instead of to me, I'll never
forgive you, Ken."

"Well, right now, I'm not planning on
selling to anybody," Ken said. "So why

don't we quit talking about this. Let's cook the corn and eat some supper."

"I'm not hungry," Kurt said, rising to his feet. He stormed out of the house.

The Aldens sat in silence. They felt bad about having heard the argument between Ken and his brother.

Ken seemed a little embarrassed about it, too. "I'm sorry you Aldens had to hear our family squabbles," he said.

Grandfather waved his hand to let Ken know it didn't matter. "I know how important it is to you to hang onto this farm," Grandfather said.

"I bought this farm with my own money, James," Ken said. "I didn't even take out a loan. I paid cash."

"I remember," Grandfather said.

"Believe it or not, Dad, Uncle Kurt and I really do have your best interests at heart. We're worried about you," David said.

"Well, stop worrying," Ken said. "What's best for me is to stay right here and keep farming my land."

"I wish I was as sure of that as you are,"

David said. He picked up his briefcase and gave his father a hug.

"I need to get home," David said. As he was leaving, he noticed the red cap sitting on the counter.

"Hey, I was wondering what happened to my cap," he said, picking it up.

Jessie looked up. "You mean that cap belongs to you?" she asked.

"Yes. I just got it a couple weeks ago. It's got a light on it, see?" He flipped the switch and the bulb lit up. "I was really upset when I noticed it was missing this morning."

The Aldens all looked at each other. "We found it in the maze this morning," Henry said.

"You did?" David sounded surprised. "Gee, I wonder how it got there." He scratched his head. "Now that I think about it, I remember I borrowed a rake from the shed the other night. I'll bet I left it in the shed then."

"How did it get from the shed to the middle of the maze?" Jessie wondered.

"That's a mystery, isn't it," David said

with a smile. "I just know I didn't put it there. I haven't been in the maze for days."

"Maybe the person who dumped the manure in the maze went into the shed to get a shovel or something and found it," Violet suggested.

"Maybe," David said. "In fact, maybe they left it in the maze on purpose so you'd think *I* was the vandal."

"I would never think that, Son," Ken said.

David smiled again. "I hope not." He picked up his cap. "Well, I'd better be going. See you all later."

After a hearty supper, the Aldens decided to take a walk through the maze before bed. It was just starting to get dark, so they borrowed flashlights from Ken. Ken and Grandfather sat on rocking chairs on the back porch.

"I wonder how David's cap got from the shed to the maze," Violet said as she shined her flashlight on the path ahead of them.

The cornstalks rippled in the night breeze as the children turned a corner.

"Obviously someone took it out of the shed," Henry said. "But who? Who could have gotten in there?"

"It could have been anybody," Violet said. "Ken doesn't keep the shed locked."

"I'll bet Mr. Sweeney goes in there a lot," Jessie said.

Henry could see the light from Mr. Sweeney's trailer through the cornstalks. "He lives here, so it would be pretty easy for him to sneak into the maze at night when no one's watching," Henry said.

"What about Peggy Rodman?" Benny asked. "She lives pretty close. It wouldn't be very hard for her to sneak in during the night, either."

"Plus, she wanted to buy this land," Jessie said. "Ken said it used to belong to her family."

"He also said this maze is the one thing that's preventing him from selling his farm right now," Henry said. "So maybe she thinks Ken will sell if he doesn't have his maze anymore."

"Peggy Rodman isn't the only person

who wants to buy this farm," Benny said. "Kurt wants to buy it, too."

"But Kurt is Ken's brother," Violet pointed out. "I don't think he'd vandalize his brother's property."

Jessie sighed. "I think we've got too many suspects and not enough clues."

"More clues," said Benny, "that's what we need. More clues and . . . " He grinned. "More corn!"

CHAPTER 6

Noises in the Night

Swish! Swish!

Benny opened one eye. What was that noise?

He peered at the clock that sat on the bedside table between him and Henry. It read 3:04 A.M.

Swish! Swish! Crack!

It was a warm night, and all the windows were open. Whatever it was, the noise was coming from outside.

"Benny? Are you awake?" Henry whispered.

"Yes," Benny said nervously. He turned to Henry. "I hear something outside."

"I hear it, too," Henry said. "Let's go see what it is."

The boys got up and went over to the window. Something was moving at the far corner of the maze, but the boys couldn't tell what it was.

There was a soft knock at the bedroom door.

"It's Jessie and Violet," Jessie whispered through the closed door. "We think there's someone in the maze!"

"We know," Henry said as Benny opened the door. "The noise woke us up, too."

Violet flipped on the hall light. "I think we should wake Grandfather and Ken and see what's going on."

"Good thinking," Henry said. He went to knock on Ken's door while Jessie knocked on Grandfather's door.

"Wake up! There's someone in the maze!" Henry and Jessie said at the same time.

Grandfather and Ken both came out of

their rooms. Grandfather wore a blue bathrobe over his pajamas. Ken wore a white bathrobe and leaned on his cane.

"What's going on?" Grandfather asked

"We don't know," Jessie said. "We heard noises outside. When we looked out the window, we saw something moving in the maze."

"Let's go check it out," Ken said.

Everyone padded down the stairs. Ken grabbed a flashlight from the kitchen drawer, then turned on the back porch light. The night air felt warm as the Aldens stepped out onto the porch.

The swishing noise was much louder outside. The Aldens peered into the darkness, waiting for their eyes to adjust. It sounded like . . . someone was chopping down the cornstalks!

Henry and Grandfather hurried toward the maze.

The noise stopped.

"Hello?" Grandfather called. "Is anyone there?"

"Oh, no!" Henry groaned as they drew

closer to the maze.

Someone had indeed chopped down part of it.

Just then, a dark figure emerged from the gaping hole in the rows of corn. The person was wearing a ski mask and a hood and carried something in his hand. He took one look at Henry and Grandfather, then bolted in the opposite direction.

"Hey, stop!" Henry called. He ran after the intruder. Jessie, Violet, and Benny were close behind.

They chased the person around the side of the house toward the road. It was so dark they couldn't see the person, but they could still hear running footsteps.

In the distance they heard a car or truck start up and drive away.

"We lost him," Violet said mournfully. The Aldens stopped running. Jessie put her hands on her knees to try to catch her breath.

"Maybe not," Henry said, his chest heaving. "Listen! I still hear footsteps!"

The others heard the footsteps, too.

"Come on!" Jessie said. They all started running again. They ran in the direction of the footsteps . . . straight into Mr. Sweeney.

The Aldens came to an abrupt halt.

"What are you kids doing up at this hour?" Mr. Sweeney asked gruffly. He wore a dark hooded sweatshirt over dark pajamas.

"There was someone in the maze," Jessie explained.

"Someone was cutting down the corn-stalks," Benny put in.

"We saw him running this way, so we followed him," Henry said.

Mr. Sweeney nodded. "I followed him, too. Is Ken up?"

"Yes," Henry replied. "I think he and Grandfather are in the maze."

They all trooped back around the corner. Grandfather and Ken were inspecting the damage with flashlights. Ken held a piece of paper in his hand.

"What's that?" Benny asked.

"It's another note," Ken said. He handed it to Henry.

"It's just like the last one," Jessie said.

Letters from magazine headlines had been cut out and pasted to the paper. The message read: CANCEL THE KING CORN DAYS FESTIVAL OR ELSE!

"Or else what?" Violet whispered.

"I don't think I want to find out," Ken said. He rubbed the back of his neck. "Perhaps I should cancel the festival."

"What?" Jessie cried.

"You can't do that!" Violet and Benny exclaimed.

Mr. Sweeney took a few steps into the maze, put his hands on his hips, and looked around.

"I don't think you've got much choice but to cancel," Mr. Sweeney told Ken. "One whole section of the field is gone. It's been cut down. I don't know how we can repair the damage this time."

Ken shook his head sadly. "I just don't understand this. Why would somebody want to destroy my maze? Why would somebody want me to cancel the festival?"

"You have absolutely no idea who might be behind this, Ken?" Jessie pressed.

"None at all."

"Mr. Sweeney, did you get a good look at the intruder?" Henry asked.

"It was too dark," Mr. Sweeney said.

"We know one thing about him," Benny said.

"What's that?" Violet asked.

"He sure can run fast," Benny said. "I'm exhausted!"

"You're exhausted because it's still the middle of the night," Grandfather said.

Ken sighed. "There isn't much we can do right now," he said. "Maybe we should all try to get some more sleep. In the morning we'll see how bad the damage is."

The Aldens agreed, and they all trooped back into the house.

Violet got Benny a glass of water, and Henry and Jessie tucked him in.

"How come we didn't see Mr. Sweeney out back by the maze?" Benny asked. "We saw the bad person, but we didn't see Mr. Sweeney."

"That's a good question, Benny," Jessie said. "Mr. Sweeney was chasing the person, too. But he got around the house before we did. It seems like either Mr. Sweeney should have been far enough ahead of us to catch the intruder or we should have seen Mr. Sweeney chasing the intruder, too."

"It was dark," Violet said. "It's so hard to know what really happened." The other children nodded.

"Maybe we should talk to Mr. Sweeney in the morning," Henry said.

Benny looked a little nervous. "Do you think the bad person will be back tonight?" he asked.

"I don't think so, Benny," Jessie said.

"He's done enough damage for one night," Henry added. "Besides, he knows we're on the case!"

Benny grinned. "And we'll solve it!"

CHAPTER 7

Too Many Loose Ends

The Alden children slept until almost nine o'clock the next morning. When they got up, the house was quiet.

"I wonder where Grandfather and Ken are," Benny said.

"Maybe they're downstairs," Henry said. So the children headed downstairs.

They heard a voice in the living room. Assuming it was Ken, they followed the voice.

But it wasn't Ken's voice they heard; it was David's.

He was talking on the telephone.

"Yeah, I think he's pretty shaken up," David said in a low voice as he straightened his tie. "One or two more scares like this and he'll be ready to sell. I can almost guarantee it."

David jumped when he saw the Aldens. He quickly picked up a magazine that was lying on the couch. "I'll have to call you back," he said into the phone. Then he hung up.

"We didn't mean to intrude," Violet said. "We were looking for our grandfather."

"And Ken," Benny added.

"You didn't intrude," David said with a stiff smile as he stuffed the magazine into the front pocket of his briefcase. "I was just talking to my wife. Dad and your grandfather went into town to do a little shopping. They left rolls and juice for you in the kitchen."

"Did you hear about what happened last night?" Jessie asked.

"Yes," David replied. "It's a shame, isn't it?" He checked his watch. "Goodness!

Look at the time! I'd better run."

He picked up his briefcase and hurried for the front door. "Don't forget the rolls and juice!" he said. And then he was gone.

The children looked at each other. "He sure was in a hurry to leave," Jessie said.

"Did you see that magazine he shoved into his briefcase?" Henry asked. "I got the impression he didn't want us to see it."

"I wonder why," Violet said.

"Maybe it had letters cut out of the headlines," Benny suggested.

"Do you think David could be the one vandalizing Ken's maze?" Jessie asked.

"I don't think so," Violet replied. "David is Ken's son. He wouldn't hurt his own father any more than Kurt would hurt his own brother."

"But he's worried about his father," Jessie pointed out. "He wants Ken to sell his farm and move into town, but Ken won't do that. He doesn't want to give up the maze or the festival, even though they're a lot of work. Maybe this is the only way David can get Ken to move into town."

"Maybe David and Kurt are working together to get Ken to sell the farm," Jessie suggested.

"That's an interesting possibility, Jessie," Henry said, tapping his finger to his chin.

"The cap with the light belonged to David," Benny pointed out. "And David's always carrying a magazine."

"But he's always so well-dressed," Violet said. "It's hard to imagine him mucking around a field full of manure."

"Maybe Kurt dumped the manure," Jessie said.

"I don't think so," Henry said. "The person we saw last night could run really fast. I don't think Kurt could run that fast."

"Mr. Sweeney can run fast," Benny said.

"Yes, he can," Jessie agreed. "We were going to talk to him some more today."

"Right," Henry said. "Let's get some breakfast and then go and do that."

The children ate a quick breakfast of toast and cereal, then headed to the barn.

"I really don't have a lot of time for chit-chat," Mr. Sweeney said as he carried a bucket of feed to the chicken coop. "I've got work to do."

The Aldens trailed along behind him.

"We know you're busy," Jessie said. "We just wanted to ask you a couple of questions about last night."

"Well, make it quick," Mr. Sweeney said. He dumped the bucket of feed onto the ground in front of the clucking chickens. The chickens all waddled over and pecked at the food.

"We were just wondering what you were doing in the front yard last night?" Henry asked.

Mr. Sweeney scowled. "Same as you," he said. "Trying to catch the guy who was prowling around the maze. I told you that last night."

"But we didn't see you by the maze. How did you get around to the front of the house so quickly?" Jessie asked.

"And how come you didn't catch the guy?" Benny asked.

Mr. Sweeney glared at the children. "You think I'm the one who's vandalizing the maze? Is that what you're saying?"

"Oh, no, Mr. Sweeney," Violet said right away. She would never accuse anyone unless she was sure. And they still weren't sure of anything.

"We're just trying to figure out what happened. That's all," Jessie said.

"Maybe you saw something we didn't," Benny said.

Mr. Sweeney scratched his neck. "Well, I thought I heard something out in the field around three o'clock this morning," he said. "So I got up and went to check it out. But I didn't see or hear anything unusual. I was about to go back inside when I heard a car out on the road."

The group strolled back toward the barn. "It sounded as if the car was stopped right in front of the house," Mr. Sweeney went on. "So I went around front to see who it was. That was about the time you folks came outside. I saw a dark figure run past, so I tried to catch him, but he got away. Then you kids caught up to me. That's all I know."

"Can you describe the car you saw?"

Henry asked. "We never saw it."

"I didn't see it, either. I only heard it. By the time I got to the road, it was gone."

"Too bad," Benny said.

"So, did our intruder get away on foot or in a car?" Jessie wondered.

"I don't know," Mr. Sweeney said. "Right now we have to think about the maze. I was looking at it this morning, trying to figure out whether the damage could be repaired."

The Aldens were surprised Mr. Sweeney had thought about repairing the maze at all. He hadn't sounded very hopeful about repairing it last night.

"Can it be repaired?" Violet asked.

"Come see what you think." Mr. Sweeney led them over to the field.

Jessie gasped when she saw the damage.

"Oh no," Violet said.

A whole section had been chopped down. Pieces of cornstalk and ears of corn lay scattered on the ground.

"Of course, if it was up to me, I'd just cancel the festival," Mr. Sweeney said. "But Ken won't want to cancel."

"No, he won't," Jessie agreed.

"So, I was thinking I could put up a fence to show where the path is supposed to be. What do you think?" Mr. Sweeney asked.

"That might work," Henry said.

"You could paint the fence green so it blends in with the rest of the field," Violet suggested.

"Maybe you could even attach some of these corncobs that are all over the ground to the fence," Benny said. "Then it would still be sort of a corn maze."

Mr. Sweeney scratched his chin. "It'll be a lot of work," he said. "If I'm going to do all that before the festival this weekend, I'm going to need some help." He looked at the children.

"We'll help you, Mr. Sweeney," Benny said right away.

"That's right," Violet added. "Anything for Ken and the King Corn Days Festival."

"Well, it looks like Ken and your grand-father are back from town. Why don't you go see what Ken has to say about our plans," Mr. Sweeney said. "I'll go get my tools. And I'll meet you back here in a bit."

When the Aldens walked up to the house, they noticed Kurt's rusty blue pickup parked next to Grandfather's rented van. As soon as the children stepped inside the house, they could hear the two brothers bickering.

"Someone tried to chop down your field? I don't like this, Ken," Kurt said. "I don't like it at all."

"Well, what do you want me to do?" Ken responded.

"You know what I want you to do. I want you to sell the farm and move into town. I'll give you a good price—"

"I will not be run off my own land!" Ken shouted. "Besides, what makes you so sure you wouldn't have the same troubles I'm having?"

"I know I wouldn't," Kurt said. "All of your troubles are related to that maze. I'll just tear the maze down."

Ken grit his teeth. "That's exactly why I won't sell to you," he replied.

Henry cleared his throat. "Hello, Ken. Hello, Kurt," he said cautiously.

The older men glanced at the children, then turned away from each other.

"Hello, kids," Ken said without a lot of enthusiasm.

Kurt yawned and stretched. Then he stood up. "Gosh, I could use another cup of coffee. I sure am tired today."

"Why are you so tired?" Violet asked.

"I don't know," Kurt said as he poured himself a cup of coffee. "I didn't sleep very well last night. What have you kids been up to this morning?"

"Talking to Mr. Sweeney," Benny said. "He thinks we can repair the maze." The children told Ken and Kurt what they and Mr. Sweeney had decided.

"You don't mind if some of the paths are marked by a fence instead of by corn, do you, Ken?" Violet asked.

"Well, ideally a corn maze should be all corn," Ken said. "But if the choice is a maze with a little fencing here and there or no maze, I'll choose the fencing."

Jessie smiled. "That's what we thought you'd say."

"We told Mr. Sweeney we'd help him build the fences," Benny said.

"Thank you, kids. I sure do appreciate all the work you're doing on the farm. This is supposed to be your vacation and it seems like all you're doing is working."

"But this kind of work is fun," Violet said.

Just as they were turning to leave, Benny noticed a nasty jagged cut on Kurt's arm.

"Kurt, what happened to your arm?" Benny asked.

"What? Oh, that," Kurt pushed up the sleeve of his black hooded sweatshirt and looked at the cut. "I was uh . . . taking out an old barbed wire fence last night. I must have cut it then."

"That rusty old fence down by the creek?" Ken cried.

"That's the one," Kurt replied.

"By yourself?" Ken asked.

"Sure. Why not?" Kurt said with a shrug. Ken snorted. "You're not that much younger than I am, Kurt. And apparently you're not as smart as I am, either. What are you thinking taking on a big job like that by yourself?"

Kurt shrugged. "I can handle it," he said.

"That looks like a bad cut," Violet said with concern.

"When was your last tetanus shot?" Ken asked.

Kurt scowled. "Will you quit treating me like a child? I'm fine!"

"Why don't you let Jack come over and help you finish with that fence," Ken suggested.

"That won't be necessary," Kurt said. "The job's done. Now if you don't mind, I think I'll head home. I've got things to do."

Kurt plopped his hat on his head, then headed out the back door.

Ken just sat at the table and shook his head. "Stubborn old coot," he muttered.

"You and Kurt sure argue a lot," Benny said.

Ken looked surprised. "Yes, I guess we do," he said. "We've always argued. Ever since we were little kids. We're still at it."

"Why?" Violet asked.

Ken shrugged. "I don't know. We're both stubborn. And I think deep down, we both like arguing."

The Aldens frowned. It was hard to understand why brothers would *enjoy* arguing!

CHAPTER 8

The Blue Pickup

The Aldens worked on the maze for most of the day. Mr. Sweeney cut posts of wood, then Violet and Benny lined them up where they needed to go. Henry and Jessie stapled chicken wire fencing from post to post. And everyone attached cornstalks into the chicken wire. The maze wouldn't be perfect, but at least it would be open in time for the festival on Saturday.

Jessie pounded in another post, then tucked her hair behind her ear. She glanced at the cornstalks beside her. "Did you notice how thick these stalks are?"

"They're pretty thick," Violet agreed as she dropped another cut post next to Henry.

"I wonder what the person last night used to chop them down?" Jessie asked.

Henry stapled chicken wire to Jessie's post. "Probably a machete," he said.

"A machete must be pretty sharp," Jessie said, "to cut through a plant that's so thick."

"You'd get a pretty nasty cut from one if you weren't careful," Henry said.

"Kurt had a pretty nasty cut," Benny pointed out.

"He said he got it from an old barbed wire fence," Violet said. "Do you think he could be lying?"

"I don't know," Benny said.

Mr. Sweeney came up behind the children. "I need to go into town and get some more chicken wire," he said. "We don't have quite enough to finish the job."

"Would you like us to go with you, Mr. Sweeney?" Violet asked.

"No. Why don't you finish up what you're doing. Then you can take a break until I get back," he said.

The Aldens used up all the chicken wire they had left, then they decided to take a walk and talk some more about the mystery.

"Even though some of the clues point to Kurt and David, I just don't think it's either of them," Violet said. "They're Ken's family. Family members don't hurt each other."

"I hope not, Violet," Henry said. "But think about it. Either one of them could have come over and toilet-papered the maze during the night. We know the cap with the light belongs to David. This morning, David said he was talking to his wife, but he could have been talking to Kurt. Remember, he said, 'One more scare like this and he'll be ready to sell.' And now this cut of Kurt's seems awfully suspicious."

The Aldens found themselves walking down the hill toward Peggy Rodman's place. She was outside working in her vegetable garden. A wheelbarrow of zucchini stood beside her.

"Hello, Ms. Rodman," Violet said politely.

Peggy looked up at the Aldens, squinting in the sun. She frowned. "You're the kids who are staying with Ken Johnson, aren't you?" she asked.

"Yes," Jessie replied.

"Too bad about the festival on Saturday," Peggy said as she tossed another zucchini into the wheelbarrow.

"What do you mean?" Henry asked.

"Well, the festival is cancelled, isn't it?" Peggy asked. She held her hand to her forehead to shade her eyes. "I heard about the trouble up at Ken's place last night. I heard part of the maze was completely destroyed."

"We're helping to fix it," Benny said.

"Ken said the festival will go on as scheduled on Saturday," Jessie added.

"Really?" Peggy looked surprised. "Boy, Ken just doesn't give up, does he?"

"Nope," Benny said.

"Well, have a nice day," Henry said.

The Aldens were about to continue walking when Peggy said something that stopped them in their tracks. "Did you all hear that noisy truck that came roaring down the road during the night?"

"You heard a truck during the night?" Jessie asked.

"Anybody within ten miles of here had to have heard it," Peggy declared. "Whoever it was, the cops ought to take away his driver's license. The guy was probably driving about eighty miles an hour."

"What time was that?" Henry asked.

"About three-thirty in the morning," Peggy replied.

That was just after the Aldens and Ken had woken up and gone outside.

"Did you get a good look at the truck or was it too dark?" Benny asked.

"Well, I could tell when it went under that street light over there that it was blue," Peggy said, pointing at a street light over by the road. "And I noticed one of the headlights was out. But that's all I saw."

"I wonder if the person who destroyed part of Ken's maze got away in that truck," Violet said.

"Well, if you find a blue truck that's got a headlight out, you might want to talk to the owner," Peggy said.

As the Aldens walked away, Benny said, "We know somebody who has a blue truck. I don't know if they've got a headlight burned out. But they definitely have a blue truck."

"Kurt," the others said at the same time.

"I think we'd better pay a visit to Kurt," Jessie said.

Mr. Sweeney was still gone when the children returned to Ken's. Grandfather and Ken were in the middle of a game of chess.

"Does Kurt live very far away?" Henry asked.

"His is the next farm up the road," Ken replied. "It's about a mile away. Why?"

"We were thinking we'd like to visit him," Jessie said. "Would that be all right?" She didn't want to tell Ken why they wanted to visit Kurt. Not until they were sure about their suspicions.

"That would be fine," Ken said as he moved a pawn forward. "You might enjoy looking around his farm. Just don't tell him I said so." Ken winked.

"Be back in time for supper," Grandfather said.

"We will," Violet promised.

The children set off. They trudged up one hill, then down the other side. When they came to the top of the next hill, they saw a tall white farmhouse in the valley below. It looked a lot like Ken's house, only smaller.

"That must be Kurt's house," Benny said, pointing.

A familiar rusty blue pickup truck sat under the shade of a large maple tree. As the Aldens drew closer, they noticed the right headlight was smashed in.

"Oh, no," Violet moaned when she saw the broken headlight.

"Let's go talk to Kurt," Henry said.

As the Aldens approached the house, they heard a strange noise. It lasted a few seconds, then stopped. Then it started again.

"What's that noise?" Jessie asked.

"It sounds like a machine gun," Benny

said. The noise was coming from the front porch.

The children approached the porch very cautiously.

"It's Kurt!" Henry said with a short laugh. "He's snoring."

Kurt was lying on his back on a padded wicker sofa. He was sound asleep.

"Should we wake him?" Violet whispered.

But before anyone could answer, Kurt's eyes flew open. "What?" he said, startled. "What's the matter?"

"Oh, it's you," Kurt said when his eyes focused on the Aldens. He rubbed his eyes and smiled. "I'm afraid you caught me."

"Caught you?" Violet asked.

"Caught me sleeping in the middle of the day," Kurt said. He sat up. "But I'm awake now. What brings you kids up here on such a nice day?"

The children climbed the porch steps and stood around in an awkward semicircle.

"We heard a car or truck out by the road last night right after we chased the person who was trying to destroy the maze," Henry began.

"You heard a vehicle in the middle of the night? On our quiet little road?" Kurt looked surprised.

"Yes," Jessie said. "We also talked to your neighbor, Peggy Rodman."

Kurt scowled when Jessie mentioned Peggy's name.

"She heard it, too," Jessie went on. "In fact, she said she even saw the vehicle."

Jessie watched Kurt carefully. "She said she saw a blue pickup truck that was missing a headlight."

"Hmm," Kurt said, glancing over at his truck. "I have a blue pickup that's missing a headlight."

The Aldens waited for him to say more.

"I suppose you're wondering whether it was my truck that Ms. Rodman saw?" Kurt asked.

"Yes," Jessie said.

Kurt took a deep breath, then let it out. "Okay, I admit I was out late last night. But it's not what you think."

He shifted on the sofa. "I didn't destroy Ken's maze. I would never do anything to hurt my brother. I was trying to help him."

"Help him how?" Violet asked. "What were you doing?"

"I'm worried about Ken," Kurt said. "Somebody really wants him to cancel the festival. Whoever it is, I'm afraid that person could be dangerous. So last night I took my truck and parked on the road next to Ken's. Then I waited. I wanted to see if anyone came onto the property."

"And did you see the intruder?" Henry wanted to know.

"Unfortunately, I fell asleep," Kurt said. "I didn't wake up until you folks started chasing him."

"That's too bad," Benny said.

"Yes, but I saw him run across the road and into the cornfield across the way," Kurt said. Then he disappeared.

"Did you get a good look at him?" Henry asked.

"Not good enough. He was wearing a dark shirt and pants. And it looked like he had a hood of some kind over his head."

"That was all we saw, too," Violet said.

"I know the road that runs on the other side of that field," Kurt went on. "It goes behind Peggy Rodman's place. So I took off as fast as I could, hoping I'd catch him coming out the other side. But by the time I got over there, he was gone."

"That's why you were so tired this morning," Violet said. "You really were up most of the night."

"Yes."

"So why didn't you just tell us that's what you'd been doing this morning?" Jessie asked.

Kurt smiled. "I didn't want Ken to know I'd been staking out his place like some sort of undercover detective," he said. "He would've been angry. He'd have said I should mind my own business."

"He probably would have," Henry agreed. "Ken likes to take care of himself."

Later, when the children were walking back to Ken's, Jessie said, "Well, that explains the blue truck that Peggy saw."

"We aren't any closer to solving this case than we ever were," Benny grumbled.

"This is a tough one," Henry agreed. "But we'll figure it out."

"At least the festival will go on," Violet said.

"Unless our intruder shows up again," Jessie said.

CHAPTER 9

Trouble!

When the Aldens returned to Ken's, Mr. Sweeney was back. He was just finishing up the last of the repair work in the maze.

"Tomorrow we paint the fence posts," Violet said.

"And decorate for the festival," Benny added.

"Can you kids help me go down all the paths right now and make sure the rest of the maze is in good shape?" asked Mr. Sweeney.

"Sure," the Aldens replied.

They divided up—Mr. Sweeney, Henry, and Violet, and Jessie and Benny—and headed down different paths.

"Everything looks good over here," Jessie called after a little while.

"Here, too," Henry called back.

"Wait a minute," Violet said. "What's that?"

A round black object had caught her eye. Violet and Henry rushed down the path to see what it was.

"A tire?" Violet said with surprise. The tire was short and fat.

"It's too small to have come from a car," Henry said.

"What else could it have come from?" Violet asked.

"I don't know," Henry said as Mr. Sweeney, Jessie, and Benny came up behind them. "Maybe a wagon?"

Mr. Sweeney picked up the tire. There was another note underneath. Henry picked it up. Like the other notes that had been found in the maze, it was written in letters

cut from magazine or newspaper headlines. "CANCEL THE FESTIVAL OR THERE WILL BE TROUBLE," Jessie read over Henry's shoulder.

"Oh, no," Violet said.

"What kind of trouble?" Benny asked.

"I don't know," Mr. Sweeney said grimly. "But this looks like a tire from the trailer we use for hayrides. I'd better go see if the trailer is okay."

The children followed Mr. Sweeney through the maze and over to the barn.

Mr. Sweeney grabbed a tire iron from a workbench in the corner, then went around and checked each tire on the trailer.

"They're all tight," Mr. Sweeney said after he'd checked the last one.

"So what does the note mean?" Benny asked.

"Maybe it means the person hasn't actually done anything yet, but they're planning on doing something to the tires sometime before the festival," Henry said.

Violet gasped. "That sounds dangerous!"

"We'd better show this note and tire to

Ken and Grandfather," Jessie said. She and Henry picked up the tire and trooped up to the house.

They found Ken and Grandfather making dinner in the kitchen. Grandfather was peeling potatoes. Ken was snapping beans at the kitchen table. A beef roast rotated slowly in the rotisserie on the counter.

Ken looked up curiously as Mr. Sweeney and the children walked in. When he saw the worried faces, he asked, "Is something the matter?"

"We may have some more trouble," Mr. Sweeney said, pointing to the tire.

Ken looked at the tire. "I don't understand," he said.

Henry showed him the note.

"Th-this sounds like a threat!" Ken said angrily. He looked at the children. "Where did you get this?"

"We found it in the maze," Violet said. "It was down one of the dead-end paths."

"Do you suppose the person who was hacking down the corn put it there last night?" Jessie asked.

"It wasn't there this morning," Mr. Sweeney said. "I walked through the whole maze looking for damage. If this note and wheel were there then, I would've seen them."

"So somebody must have put them in there today while you were shopping for chicken wire and we were out walking or visiting Kurt. That's the only time the maze was unguarded," Jessie said.

"I'm guessing it's the same person who tried to destroy the maze last night. Now we're being warned there's going to be trouble if the festival goes on as planned," Henry said.

"Did you see anyone around, Ken?" Violet asked.

"No," Ken replied. "James and I were playing chess all afternoon."

"David stopped by for a few minutes," Grandfather said. "I wonder if he saw anything?"

The children exchanged looks. If David had stopped by, they wondered, could *he* have left the wheel and the note?

"I'm worried," Ken said, shaking his head. "What if this person makes good on his threat? What if he loosens one of the wheels on the trailer and the trailer tips over? People could get hurt."

He slumped back against his chair in defeat. "I think I'm going to have to cancel the festival," he said sadly.

"No!" the Aldens said together.

"I'm sorry, kids," Ken said. "But I don't see any other choice. I can't take a chance on someone getting hurt."

"Should I call the radio station so they can make an announcement about the festival being canceled?" Mr. Sweeney asked. "We don't want people driving out here for nothing."

"It's a little late to do that today," Ken said. "The office is probably only open until five o'clock. But if you'd take care of that for me tomorrow, I'd appreciate it."

Mr. Sweeney nodded.

"So that gives us less than twenty-four hours to solve this case," Henry said glumly.

"If we figure out who's doing this, you

won't have to cancel the festival, will you, Ken?" Violet asked.

"No," Ken said. "But do you really think you can catch someone so quickly?"

"We'll sure try," Henry said.

"We know one thing for sure," Jessie said after supper. The sun was going down, but the children sat on bales of hay behind the barn reviewing all the clues they had.

"What?" Benny asked, swinging his feet.

Jessie pulled her legs up onto the bale she was sitting on. "We know that it couldn't have been Kurt who put the tire in the maze," she said. "We were with him this afternoon."

"Not the whole time," Henry pointed out. "We walked down to Peggy's first."

"But we woke Kurt up when we got to his house," Jessie said. "I don't think he would've had time to drive up here, hide a tire in the maze, then drive back home and fall asleep."

"You're probably right, Jessie," Violet said.

"Mr. Sweeney could have done it,"

Henry said. "He was here by himself for a little while before we got back."

"David was here, too," Benny put in.

"But David is Ken's son," Violet said. She still couldn't believe he was involved in all this.

"How about Peggy Rodman?" Jessie suggested. "Kurt said that the person who ran away from Ken's house last night went into the field across the street. And that field comes out down by Peggy's house."

"Maybe we should do what Kurt did last night," Benny said.

"What do you mean, Benny?" Violet asked.

Benny jumped down from his bale of hay. "Maybe we should stake out the maze and the barn tonight. Make sure nothing bad happens."

"That's a great idea, Benny!" Jessie said. "We could sit up in the lookout tower. I think we could see both the maze and the barn from up there."

"We can roll out our sleeping bags and pretend we're having a campout," Violet said. "And we can take turns keeping watch."

"If we're lucky, we'll catch the person in the act and save Ken's maze," Henry said.

"Not to mention the whole King Corn Days Festival!" Benny said.

"I don't know," Ken said a little while later when the children explained their plan. He and Grandfather were sitting in the living room paging through old photo albums and talking about things they used to do together when they were young.

"I appreciate you kids wanting to help," Ken went on. "But this sounds a little dangerous."

"We'll be careful, Ken," Violet said. "We promise."

"This might be the only way to catch the vandal," Jessie said.

"You don't want to let someone get away with this, do you?" Benny asked.

"Well, no," Ken admitted. "But I don't want to put you children in harm's way, either."

"Perhaps you and I could sit outside and

keep watch, too," Grandfather suggested. "Those back porch chairs of yours are pretty comfortable. And I know my grandchildren won't do anything foolish."

Ken looked at Grandfather. "You'd be willing to spend the night sleeping in a chair outdoors?"

"To catch the person who's been wrecking your maze?" Grandfather said. "You bet I would!"

"Then it's settled," Henry said. "We'll go get our sleeping bags."

CHAPTER 10

Stakeout!

Benny shifted in his sleeping bag. "What time is it?" he whispered.

Henry had agreed to take the first watch. Jessie, Violet, and Benny were trying to sleep, but it was hard for Jessie to get comfortable on the wood floor. And Violet and Benny were simply too excited to sleep.

Henry glanced at his watch. "It's a quarter to twelve," he whispered back.

"That's pretty late," Benny said with a yawn.

"Yes, it is," Henry agreed. He held a big

spotlight in his lap. Everyone else had small flashlights.

If Henry saw anyone around the maze, he was supposed to wake everyone up and shine the spotlight on the intruder. Ken said the light was bright enough to light up the whole yard. But so far, Henry hadn't had any reason to use it.

Jessie rolled over onto her stomach, but that wasn't any more comfortable. Finally she sat up.

"I think I'm going to move my sleeping bag down onto the grass," Jessie said. "Violet and Benny, do you want to come with me?"

"I'd rather sleep up here," Benny said.

"Me, too," Violet said.

So Jessie got up, carried her sleeping bag and pillow down the stairs, and settled herself on the grass.

"Is that better, Jessie?" Henry called to her.

"Much better," Jessie said as she snuggled down into her sleeping bag.

"It's kind of nice being out here under

the stars," Violet said, gazing up at the night sky.

"Are there more stars here than there are at home?" Benny wondered.

"No," Jessie replied. "It just looks like it because we're out in the country. There are no city lights to block out some of the dimmer stars."

The children picked out the Big Dipper and the Little Dipper and the Pleiades.

Then, one by one, they drifted off to sleep.

After a while, Henry tiptoed down the stairs with his flashlight and nudged Jessie. "Can you take over the watch? I'm getting tired."

Jessie rolled over. "Sure," she said softly. She yawned and stretched. "Have you seen anything unusual?"

"No." Henry shook his head. "I think Grandfather and Ken are sleeping now, too. I haven't heard their chairs rocking at all."

Jessie sat up where she had a good view of the maze and Henry handed her a flashlight. "Wake me up if you see anything," he said. Then he crept back up to the lookout tower.

"I will," Jessie promised.

It didn't take Henry long to fall asleep. Jessie gazed out over the yard. The moon gave off enough light so that she was sure she would see someone running across the yard.

But so far, there had been no one.

Jessie rubbed her eyes. It was hard to stay awake all by herself. Just as she was about to wake Violet, a movement at the edge of the trees caught her eye.

Jessie peered closer. A dark figure emerged from the trees. The figure crept slowly toward the maze.

Jessie pounded on the lookout tower. "Wake up!" she cried. "There's someone in the yard." She shined the flashlight toward the figure. But before Jessie could get the light focused, the person dashed into the maze.

"Quick! After him!" Henry cried.

The children flipped on their flashlights and clattered down the stairs of the lookout

tower. They raced toward the maze.

"He went in through the exit," Jessie said as the back porch light came on and Grandfather and Ken stood up.

A light went on in Jack Sweeney's trailer, too. He stepped outside. "What's going on?" he asked, pulling his robe tight around his stomach.

"Someone's in the maze," Jessie called back.

"Violet, why don't you stand guard by the entrance," Henry directed. "Benny, you stand guard by the exit. Jessie and I will see if we can corner the intruder inside the maze."

Jessie grabbed her flashlight and dashed in through the entrance. Henry hurried in through the exit. Jessie shined her flashlight on the path ahead and listened. She could hear the intruder running a few rows to her right.

The cornstalks were planted too close together for her to sneak quietly between the rows. All she could do was keep winding her way through the maze and hope that she and Henry somehow managed to corner the vandal.

Jessie saw a dark figure turn a corner and run right onto the same path she was on. The figure stopped, momentarily blinded by Jessie's flashlight. Jessie gasped when she saw who the person was.

"It's Peggy Rodman!" she yelled so everyone could hear her.

"Wait," Peggy cried, shielding her eyes. "I can explain."

Jessie hurried over to Peggy. "Let's find our way out of the maze first. Then you can explain."

"Where are you guys?" Henry called.

"I'm not sure," Jessie replied.

"I see them!" Violet cried. "I'm up in the lookout tower."

Jessie glanced up as a bright light shone down on the maze. Violet was shining the light from the lookout tower. She smiled and waved at Jessie. Jessie waved back.

"Turn right at the next intersection, Jessie," Violet called. "Then left. Then just stay on that path and you'll be out."

Jessie followed Violet's instructions. In a matter of minutes, she and Peggy were out of the maze. Ken, Jack Sweeney, Grandfather, and the other children were waiting by the exit.

Ken just stared sadly at Peggy. "So, you're the one who's been causing all my trouble," he said.

"Well, not tonight," Peggy said. "Tonight I came to look for something I'd lost. But . . . I couldn't find it." She lowered her eyes.

"Were you by any chance looking for a tire?" Mr. Sweeney asked.

"You found it already?" Peggy asked mournfully.

Jack nodded.

Peggy looked up at Ken. "I'm so sorry, Ken. I was never going to hurt anyone at the festival—not really! I just wanted to scare you. That's why I left all those notes. That's why I toilet-papered your maze and dumped the manure and yes, even left a trailer wheel.

"I know now that scaring you with that

wheel was going too far," Peggy went on. "That's why I came here tonight. I wanted to take it back before you found it. Unfortunately, I was too late." Peggy looked down at her pointy cowboy boots.

"But why would you do all this?" Ken asked, trying to make sense of what he was hearing.

"Because I wanted you to give up. I wanted you to sell your property to me and move into town. You may not know this, but your land has been in my family for three generations!"

"I do know that. Your father told me when he sold it to me," Ken said.

"He didn't think either of his daughters would want to farm," Peggy said. "But I do. I *love* farming. I've spent my whole life learning about it. Unfortunately, all I have left of my daddy's land is a little vegetable patch. And I can't even make a living from that now that you've decided to sell vegetables, too."

"I offered to let you sell your vegetables here," Ken reminded her.

"Yes, but I didn't want to just set up a little vegetable stand," Peggy said. "I could do that at home. I wanted a bigger role. I wanted to buy you out and farm this land and run the festival myself. I've been saving for years so I could make you a good offer. An offer you'd be sure to accept. But you refused."

"That must've made you really angry," Violet said.

"Yes." Peggy let out a deep breath. "I know I handled this all wrong. Vandalizing your maze is not going to convince you to sell to me. I'll pay for all the damage. And if you want to press charges—"

"I'll have to think about that," Ken said. "Right now, it's late. We're all tired. And we've got a big day tomorrow if we're going to get ready for the festival on Saturday."

Peggy nodded. "I want you to know, Ken, I really am sorry." Then she left.

Mr. Sweeney turned to go back to his trailer.

"I had no idea how much this land meant

to Peggy," Ken said, shaking his head. "That doesn't excuse what she did, but I understand why she did it."

"At least the vandalism is over," Grandfather said. "Is everybody ready for bed?"

"Can we still sleep outside for the rest of the night?" Benny wanted to know.

"Sure," Grandfather replied. "There won't be any more trouble tonight. But if you don't mind, I think Ken and I will move inside where there are real beds."

The next day, The King Corn Days Festival went on as scheduled. Visitors started arriving just before noon.

The children and Mr. Sweeney had done a good job repairing the damaged section of the maze. They had painted the wood posts green and stuck bunches of corncobs inside the chicken wire fencing. At first glance, the visitors didn't even notice that part of the maze was missing.

The children had also set up a smaller maze of hay bales for little kids. Violet had spread construction paper, markers, and scissors over several picnic tables for children who wanted to make crafts.

Kurt brought over bushels of sweet corn, which he and Ken boiled in large pots over an open fire. Henry and Jessie served up the corn as fast as it was ready, then husked more to be boiled.

"What a great festival!" Jessie said as she watched all the people milling about Ken's farm.

"People seem to be enjoying themselves," Grandfather said.

Grownups chatted with one another while their children scampered over the bales of hay and chased each other through the maze.

Families strolled about the farm, playing games, feeding the animals, and of course, munching sweet corn.

"I can't thank you children enough for all your help," Ken said. "Not only did you help get ready for the festival, you helped clean up after the vandalism all week. And you caught the vandal."

"We were happy to help," Henry said.

"Well, this festival never would've gone

on today without you," Ken said as he rolled a few ears of cooked corn in a pan of hot melted butter.

"We're all grateful to you," Kurt put in.

"We're just glad the festival didn't have to be canceled," Violet said.

When all the people went home, the Aldens helped Ken, Kurt, and Mr. Sweeney clean up. Even Peggy stopped by to see if she could help. She looked a little nervous standing in the driveway, waiting for Ken's answer.

"Sure you can," Ken said, waving her forward. "In fact, I'd like to talk to you again."

"Oh?" Peggy said warily. "H-have you decided to press charges?"

"No," Ken said. "This is something else. I know my brother and my son are worried about me. And I know this maze and festival require a lot of extra work each year. More than Jack really has time for."

Jack nodded.

"So," Ken looked at Peggy. "I was thinking, since you enjoy farming so much, maybe you'd like to help me with the maze and the festival next year?"

Peggy looked surprised. "Really?"

"There's going to come a day when I'm too old to run my farm," Ken went on. "That day hasn't come yet, but when it does, I'd sure like to sell to somebody I know will love this farm and the maze the way I do."

"But don't you want to buy Ken's farm, too, Kurt?" Benny asked.

"Shh, Benny!" Jessie scolded. "It's not our business."

"That's okay, Jessie," Kurt said. "Actually, Ken and I talked about this. I'd like to make peace with Peggy, too. Besides, I'm only five years younger than Ken. By the time he's ready to sell, I probably will be, too. And I'd sure rather sell to an individual than to a large corporation."

"I-I don't know what to say," Peggy said, her eyes growing misty.

"Say you'll do it," Kurt said.

Peggy laughed. "I'll do it."

The Aldens all smiled at each other. They liked it when things turned out well.

"So, have you started thinking about next year's maze, Ken?" Benny asked.

"It's probably a little early to be thinking about next year's maze, Jessie," Henry said.

"No, it isn't," Ken argued. "In fact, I actually have been thinking about next year's design. I'm thinking I'd like to do a boxcar . . . "

"A boxcar!" Benny cried. "Oh, boy!"

"A boxcar in honor of the Boxcar Children," Kurt said. "That sounds like a great idea, Ken."

"Can we come back next year, Grandfather?" Benny begged. "Can we? I really want to see the boxcar maze."

"Definitely, Benny," Grandfather replied. "I wouldn't miss it for all the corn in Iowa!"

GERTRUDE CHANDLER WARNER discovered when she was teaching that many readers who like an exciting story could find no books that were both easy and fun to read. She decided to try to meet this need, and her first book, *The Boxcar Children*, quickly proved she had succeeded.

Miss Warner drew on her own experiences to write the mystery. As a child she spent hours watching trains go by on the tracks opposite her family home. She often dreamed about what it would be like to set up housekeeping in a caboose or freight car— the situation the Alden children find themselves in.

While the mystery element is central to each of Miss Warner's books, she never thought of them as strictly juvenile mysteries. She liked to stress the Aldens' independence and resourcefulness and their solid New England devotion to using up and making do. The Aldens go about most of their adventures with as little adult supervision as possible—something else that delights young readers.

Miss Warner lived in Putnam, Connecticut, until her death in 1979. During her lifetime, she received hundreds of letters from girls and boys telling her how much they liked her books.